CW00496990

NECK-ROMANCER BOOK FOUR

NECK-ROMANCER
DOUBLE TROUBLE

ELIZABETH DUNLAP

This is a work of fiction. Names, characters, places, and incidents either are the product of the author's imagination or are used fictitiously, and any resemblance to any persons, living or dead, business establishments, events, or locales is entirely coincidental.

NECK-ROMANCER: DOUBLE TROUBLE

Copyright © 2021 by Elizabeth Dunlap

First Printing: Nov, 2021

Printed in the United States of America

First Edition: Nov, 2021

❀ Created with Vellum

DISCLAIMER

For Adult Audiences 18+.

Language and actions may be deemed offensive to some.

Sexually explicit content.

F/F outside of the harem.

This series includes pregnancy, and M/M relationships, men loving other men. Considering how thirsty Alec is for literally everyone in Jaz's harem, we are not surprised at all.

Trigger warnings: A heaping buttload of death. For real, be ready. Death is coming. Get the tissues. Don't say I didn't warn you <3

Jaz

I don't have a sister.

The fact has been well-established, if you've been following my story thus far.

Izzy, my supposed sister, and her girlfriend, Bailey, Sebastian's sister, sat at our table in the middle of the night. Bailey had pink skin to her brother's blue skin, and unlike him, she had pink fairy wings. She was also drop dead gorgeous.

I'm going to point out again that *I don't have a sister*, so I'm sure you can imagine the confusion coursing through my veins as I watched a blue-haired version of myself staring back at me from the other side of the table.

Alec, my warlock fiancé, had captured one of my hands, as if he was the only thing standing between me and the two women sitting across from us. Pierce, my Lycan fiancé, was on his other side, fiddling with his charmed necklace as he squinted at the girls. Sebastian, my fairy fiancé, appeared the most chill out of the four of us. I should say five of us, because Sebastian was also the physical host for my fourth fiancé, the ghost wizard, Gilbert.

Yep. That's right. I was fucking a dead person.

Sebastian had an arm slung on the back of his chair, eyeing my sister warily from where she sat beside him. "I wondered why you were keeping your girlfriend a secret, sister. I figured you were lying about having one because you were jealous about my mate."

Bailey rolled her eyes and tossed back her perfect purple hair. "There's no need to be jealous when my mate is identical to yours. Seems you can't help but have the same taste in girls as me."

"I am *so glad* my sisters aren't here," Pierce

commented with a sigh. Izzy raised her eyebrows in question. "I have five sisters."

Izzy grinned at him. Her smile was so similar to mine, but also so different at the same time. "That sounds like chaos. Can't imagine what your bathroom looks like."

"That's..." I started, but paused when she smiled at me. God, this was too weird. "That's exactly what I thought when he told me." I awkwardly tucked my hair behind my ear and stared at the ceiling.

"Izzy," Alec said, smiling despite his concern about all of this. "How about you start at the beginning. Please tell us your story."

2

Izzy

"**J**azzy!" I squealed as I ran after my sister.

She wrinkled her nose and let me catch up to her. "Don't call me Jazzy. It's bad enough that mom refuses to use our nicknames, I don't need anyone calling me Jazzy too."

I pouted, folding my little arms over my chest. "But

we're twins. We should have names that sound the same."

She groaned audibly and slumped down. "Izzyyyyyy. *Why are you like this?*"

"Cuz I'm your sister." I booped her on the nose.

I was always her shadow. She shined brightly like the sun, and I was the moon to light the darkness. Two halves of the same coin. The same face, two different hearts.

We ran through the woods behind our house, enjoying our free time before we had to leave.

At eleven years old, we were the proper age to begin our witch training.

It was finally time for us to attend Highborn.

ON THE INCANTATION EXPRESS, JAZ AND I SAT IN ONE of the compartments, our bags sitting beside us. She had a book shaped backpack, I had one with the Eeveelutions on it, both were magically expanded.

I tucked some of my long brown curls behind my ear. We had the same hair, but I always felt like mine was more wild, less tamable. I felt like a poodle.

"Are you scared?" I asked her, kicking my legs back and forth against the seat.

"Why would I be scared? Stop doing that."

I stilled and folded my hands in my lap. *I was scared.* Since I'd specialized in Divination, I was starting to get feelings. Premonitions. And I was feeling one right then, on the train, staring into my sister's brown eyes.

The feeling remained when we got to the station, when the train stopped. Jaz stood up, grabbed her bag, and waited for me to do the same. The train whistle rang in my ears. A shrill warning.

"I want to go back home," I told her. She always helped me. She was always there for me.

Jaz came over, taking my hands in hers. "Deep breaths, Izzy. We're going to school, everything will be fine."

She was wrong. I could feel it. "No, it won't. Please, go back home, Jaz."

Jaz, I'd said. Not me. *Her.*

Divination witches had a way with their words, a foreboding we didn't do on purpose. If I had been more experienced, I might've understood, but I didn't. I let Jaz lead me off the train, through Highborn Village, and up to the school.

It stood before us, the castle of Highborn Academy.

It looked wrong. Dangerous. I didn't like it.

But I trusted Jaz.

She held my hand as we went up the hill and entered the courtyard. Other witches were there, showing off their magic as they played with their friends.

Jaz's cheeks turned pink with envy. While I'd specialized already, she hadn't. For the first time, I had come in first. She marched us past everyone and into the school building.

A witch wearing long green robes stood in the foyer. She tilted her tiny spectacles to peer down at us. "The Neck twins? I'd know those curls anywhere, they're exactly like your mother's was when she was your age. I'm Professor Wisniewski."

We beamed as she gave us our room assignments and pointed us in the right direction. Jaz led me further into the school, but she paused at the bottom of the staircase.

I turned to see her staring at a group of popular kids, one in particular being a warlock with a cheeky grin on his face. He sent out illusion magic fireworks, and all the girls around him were impressed. He ate it up like pudding, flicking his short curls back.

"Jaz, let's go."

She was spellbound, dropping her foot down from the steps. "He's so *handsome*. I want to soulmate kiss him."

I gagged at the thought of kissing a boy. "No thanks. Boys are gross." I did, however, catch sight of a girl in the group, one that piqued my interest enough that I stared at her for a few seconds. She was pretty, but I didn't want to soulmate kiss her.

We watched her grab the warlock, and they kissed in front of everyone.

Jaz looked murderous. "That *hussy*." I tugged her back when she looked like she wanted to go smash the girl's face in.

"Jaz, *no*! Leave them alone. It's not like he's yours."

She tilted her chin up, that Jaz confidence spreading across her face. "He is. He's mine. I can feel it."

"You just want him because he's popular."

She scoffed, and I caught a real emotion crossing her face. She really did believe her words. Then she turned and went up the stairs, leaving me to trot behind her to keep up.

⚜

"WELL IF IT ISN'T THE LITTLE NECK TWINS."

Jaz and I looked up from our schoolwork in the library to see Candace Cauldron walking by with *him* on her arm. Alec Claus. The boy Jaz couldn't stop drooling over.

Candace knew Jaz fancied her older boyfriend, and she liked flaunting it in my sister's face.

"Getting your little studying done, I see?" She said 'studying' like it was something only extreme nerds did. "We'll be over there, making out. I do love the taste of older boys."

Eww. She was so gross. I can't believe I thought she was pretty.

I gagged as they walked away, and Jaz wilted like a dead flower once they couldn't see her. "You should forget about him. He's a loser if he doesn't want you." But she didn't hear me. She was too busy pining over Alec Claus. I turned my mp3 player on and stuck one of my earpods into her ear, the other in mine, and I clicked play on our favorite song.

BABY CAST A SPELL, I SWEAR I WON'T TELL.
Our love is all we need, to make this spell succeed.
One kiss is all it took, to know that I was hooked.
The magic in my soul, goes completely out of control.
I can't keep it in, so baby let's begin.
Baby cast a spell, I swear I won't tell.
Your love it makes me high, and I will never deny,
You're a part of me, all the love I see, so baby cast a spell,
I swear I won't tell.

I SIGHED IN CONTENTMENT AS AURORA'S FACE CAME onto my mp3 player screen. She was so beautiful, with her long black hair, her dark ebony skin.

"These lyrics are so stupiiiid," Jaz sang along, and I poked her in the side so she'd shut up.

Okay, maybe *I* was the only one into Aurora, but she was the biggest witch popstar, and I wanted to soulmate kiss her *so badly*.

She could cast a spell on me any day.

⚜

JAZ LAY ON THE GROUND BESIDE ME, PULLING UP fistfuls of grass in frustration. "Dang it, Izzy. We've been here for an entire year, and I haven't specialized yet. I'm never going to specialize."

I felt like a bad sister, since I'd already found my calling. I'd give it to her if I could, so she'd be happy again. I'd do anything for my sister.

"You will," I said, trying to reassure her. "You know you will. We come from a long line of witches, from both sides of our family. There's no way the Calderon bloodline would skip you."

That wasn't the only thing bothering her.

As the months went by, Alec Claus remained out of her reach, and she was becoming increasingly unhappy because of it. She was convinced, nay, *adamant*, that he was hers, but he continued to suck face with Candace Cauldron, ignoring us whenever we saw him.

I stared up at the clouds and thought that one of them looked like fairy wings. "I'm sorry he ignores you, Jaz." She stayed silent, to keep the tears at bay or pretend she didn't care. "We're only twelve years old, we're too young for soulmates."

"You know that's not true," she countered with a huff. "Our Headmistress met her soulmate at age eight. He kissed her on the cheek, and their magic responded. They've been together for forty years."

I pictured being saddled with someone, before I'd really experienced life. Before I'd gone anywhere, done anything. It sounded horrible. "Well, I don't want anyone."

Jaz giggled and poked me in a tease. "I've heard you talk about kissing Aurora often enough, so I don't believe that for one second."

Rolling onto my stomach, I tilted my head to study her features bathed in sunlight, just like she was. There was a sadness to her face, our face, that hadn't been there before. "It's just that... I've seen how much it hurts for you to not be with this Alec guy. What if you're wrong about him?"

She grinned, confident but lonely. "I'm not."

"I just can't jump into someone's arms if all they'll bring is sadness."

Jaz turned to me, the grass floating against her cheek, and she pressed her fingertip to my nose. "Izzy, my sweet baby sister."

I shoved her hand away and we giggled together.

"You're only two minutes older than me, stop rubbing it in my face."

She looked back up at the sky with that wistful smile that tore at my heart. "Love is worth every inch of pain that comes with it, Izzy."

She sounded ancient, like a two-hundred-year-old wood dwelling witch instead of my twelve-year-old sister.

Footsteps approached in the grass, and we sat up to see Professor Wisniewski walking up to us.

"Hello, girls," she greeted with a smile. "Jasmine, Headmistress Lume would like to see you in her office."

We both got up, but Wisniewski waved her hand at me when I followed my sister. "No no, not you, Isabelle. You can go back to your dormitory to wait for your sister's return. She'll be back in a few hours, not to worry."

I dutifully left my sister behind in that field.

I didn't know it would be the last time I saw her.

3

Izzy

Jaz didn't return. I waited for days. Headmistress Lume said she'd been called away, but refused to say why.

Two weeks later, Jaz's body was found in the forest beside Highborn, with wolf footprints nearby. Everyone said they had killed her, the Lycans. It was all anyone talked about.

I sat up in the stairwell, on a very high landing that people never used. I'd more than once considered jumping off of it. Life without my sister wasn't a life.

"Izzy."

Jumping in shock, I held onto the ledge and saw Alec Claus flying up to the platform.

He landed next to me and leaned against the bannister to mimic my pose. "I've been looking for you." He pushed back his hair, drawing my attention to his appearance. He hadn't brushed his short curls. His clothes were wrinkled. I may not have known him personally, but one thing I did know was Alec Claus never looked anything less than perfect. "Are your parents coming to get you?"

"Why do you care," I spat, resting my chin on the bannister. He went silent, and when I lifted my head, I beheld a sight I thought I'd never see.

Alec Claus was sobbing like a baby.

I backed away like he was a grenade about to explode on me, which he kind of was. Should I... comfort him?

"*Izzy, I've lost her.*"

My eyebrows knit together in confusion, but then it dawned on me, and I scowled at him. "You felt it too. You knew you were supposed to be with her."

"And I wasted my chance to keep her safe," he finished with a brokenhearted howl.

I shoved him against the bannister, and he let me do

it. Encouraged it. Accepted it. "I'll give you five seconds to tell me why you stayed away, why you put her in so much pain. Was it because we're not good enough for you?"

He shook his head, tear droplets falling on his wrinkled vest. "She was far too good for me, Izzy. She was perfection. It was Candace. I tried to end things with her the moment I saw Jaz for the first time. Candace threatened to hurt her. I would've endured anything to keep your sister safe. It was agony for me as well, Izzy, I swear to you I was not apathetic."

I scoffed at him, flipping my curls over my shoulder. "You can make all the excuses you want now that she's dead. You didn't save her. If you're her soulmate, you're supposed to protect her, and you *failed*."

I'd notched an arrow, and shot it straight into his heart, but I didn't care. My sister was gone. No amount of sob stories from her 'soulmate' would bring her back.

The sun was dead. Darkness would follow, and consume everything.

ONCE THE HIGH COUNCIL GOT WORD THAT LYCANS had slaughtered a student, well, it was a madhouse.

Highborn got round the clock security. Every ablebodied witch or wizard was asked to join the war. The school was plastered with propaganda posters, warning that the magical beasts would take us over if we didn't stop them first. And no one spoke against it, because after all, the enemy we'd fought for centuries had killed my sister.

Years passed. The war got worse. Terror escalated.

As I grew up, I felt like a faded flower without my sunlight. I excelled at my studies, I was a proficient witch in Divination. Gifted. Brilliant. My power level was unmatched. The praise meant nothing to me.

Nothing could bring my sister back.

Sometimes I wondered, maybe... just maybe... if I held out, maybe the witch world would be blessed with a necromancer after four hundred years. I would lull myself to sleep at night, just dreaming about it. Seeing her again. Holding my sister in my arms. Such thoughts threatened to destroy me.

When I graduated from Highborn, my life lay before me, and I had no direction. No purpose. But I needn't have worried.

Highborn was attacked by Centaurs shortly afterward, and the school was destroyed.

Our entire society fell to magical beasts. When we pushed against them, they pushed back harder, and they won.

While my parents went underground to try and rebuild our world, I went to the ruins of Highborn. The

NECK-ROMANCER: DOUBLE TROUBLE HB

NECK-ROMANCER: DOUBLE TROUBLE HB

bottom floor of the astronomy tower was salvageable, and I made a little home there with a tent and stacks of books to keep me company.

I'd been there for days when a wolf howl woke me up one night. Scrambling up, I whipped out my wand and left my tent, walking out into the rain.

Was it them? The wolves who killed my sister?

I rounded the corner of the tower and came face to face with a short man wearing a hoodie. He was the exact same height as me, but he was so ripped under his jacket, he looked huge.

Seeing my face made his light up, and he threw himself at me. I was so shocked, worried he was the Lycan I'd heard howling, that he managed to grab me.

Then he kissed me on the mouth.

The man realized his mistake just as he was about to slide his tongue between my lips, and he pulled away from me, looking as grossed out as I felt.

"Ewww, you're a *boy*," I whined.

"I'm sorry," he said over the rain. "I thought..."

And I realized. I knew exactly what he'd thought.

"She's been dead for twelve years," I told him, and he nodded, looking down so his hood covered his eyes. "Come on, my tent is dry."

I led a complete stranger into my tent, using magic to dry us while I heated some hot chocolate and passed him a cup of it. He lowered his hood, revealing long black hair and Korean features.

Without the rain, I was starting to sense him. This man wasn't human, or a wizard.

He was a Lycan.

I should've been terrified. He was in this tent with me, we were enemies. He could kill me, and no one would know. We shared a look, one that said he was thinking the same.

My mouth opened and closed as I tried to think of what to say. "Who are you? How did you know my sister?" I paused before he could answer, and I just went for it. "Are you the one who killed her?"

He looked horrified. "No, absolutely not. I'd never... I was incapable of hurting her."

Thunder sounded outside the tower, and I leaned back with a sigh.

"Okay, start at the beginning, wolf."

He blinked at me and set down his cup. "Twelve years ago, my pack was running patrols through the woods. We'd only get close to the school once or twice a year, sometimes as a test of bravery. Younger wolves could be a bit... adventurous."

"But not you?"

He half-chuckled, his grin so enchanting, it would've captured any other girl's attention. "I'm the Alpha. Or... I was. Alphas have to keep everyone in line." He leaned back against the tent and stared at his hands. "I had stopped to let my pack run ahead, following a scent, and three witches appeared in the forest. She was one of them. I only had to look at her, and I knew she belonged to me. She was everything I'd waited for..." His hands tightened into fists. "The other witches killed her right in front of me."

I found myself also forming fists, just to keep myself together. Twelve years had been a drop in the bucket to erase my pain. I still felt it like it was yesterday, like I was still on the bannister with Alec Claus.

"They left, and I came up to her. She was fading away, I couldn't save her... I sat next to her until she died."

The footprints next to Jaz's body. They weren't from her killers. They were from him.

My mouth felt bitter, and I set my drink down. "I... I'm sorry. Not a day has passed these long years where I didn't wish I could do something to bring her back. Our world died with her. Your kind brought us to ruin." I stopped, hating myself, knowing it wasn't his fault, but he still chose to smile at me.

He would've made Jaz so happy.

"There's nothing you can do?" he asked. "I hate to press, but... you're a witch."

"Yes, and there are rules on how we can practice magic. I can't bring people back from the dead. I can't go back in time..." I stopped, my entire body frozen, and I let out a strangled breath.

"What? What's wrong?" He leaned forward to check me, and I made him fall over when I shouted at the top of my lungs.

Lunging forward, I grabbed the Lycan's thick arms and squealed in excitement.

"*I can fix this.*"

⚜

IT WAS DANGEROUS MAGIC. FORBIDDEN. Uncontrollable. Something to be used only if there were no other options.

Resetting time was the most powerful magic known to witches. Even resurrection was secondary, and that was incredibly powerful magic. It wasn't just resetting time, it was resetting your reality. Going back to a point in time, and changing everything that happened after.

Pierce, the Lycan, helped me set up a lab inside the school ruins, where I studied for weeks to learn how to reset reality. It was during those weeks when I discovered what this would cost me.

You can send a single person back in time without repercussions, but resetting time came with a consequence I would've recoiled at before. Run away from. Forgotten this was even an option. But I'd lived for twelve years without the sunlight, and I was willing to pay the price.

I would be erased from all time and space.

No matter how many times I reset this reality, as far as the world was concerned, Izzy Neck was never born. I would never have existed. Jaz wouldn't know me. My parents wouldn't know me.

Pierce balked at this plan. "You can't take yourself away from her. Jaz needs you, Izzy."

"Jaz is dead," I reminded him. "If we want to save her, this is the only way. I'll stay in the shadows, I'll keep her safe. And you will too. No matter which reality I land in, you have to find her. Alec Claus too, as much as I hate that bastard."

I gathered up some supplies and started crafting the spell, drawing out a series of runes on the floor in my lab. Pierce watched me, clenching and unclenching his fists.

"Can I... could you bring me with you?"

I kept drawing, keeping my eyes on my work. "No. This spell only transports one person. I'm sorry, Pierce." Sitting back on my heels, I inspected my work, fixing a few runes here and there. "I'm not even sure this will work. From what I gather, this will take less power if I have to reset time again, but the first reset... it could drain my magic completely."

"That might kill you."

Nodding, I stood up and faced him.

Pierce was a good man. I was right, he would've made my sister very very happy. He was patient, understanding, kind. He treated me like I was family. This wolf deserved to be at Jaz's side.

"It might," I confirmed.

He studied my work, setting his jaw with determination. "Then use me. Use my strength for the spell so it won't fail."

I let out a slow breath, clenching my nails into my skin. "Pierce. You know you won't come back from that."

The look on his face tore me into shreds. "There's nothing left for me here, Izzy."

Me either.

CASTING THAT SPELL WAS LIKE BEING BURNED ALIVE. I rose like a phoenix from the ashes, the pain inside me turning my hair fully blue.

I used to wonder before that, why my trauma never showed on the outside. Why I hadn't sprouted tattoos, why my hair was still brown, when my entire world had been destroyed. But once that spell was cast, it all came to the surface, turning my hair as blue as the night sky.

When the magic died down, the spell working its

way through every part of my body, I stared at the ground where Pierce lay, feeling my soul die even more.

He disappeared. The lab disappeared as the castle rebuilt itself around me. My body started to shrink down until I was a little eleven-year-old girl again. Even though I was erased, my soul was still bound to hers. We would always be the same age, no matter which reality I went to.

I shouldered my bag and marched forward, to my new future.

🐲

JAZ DIED AGAIN.

I came to her before it happened, I even found Alec and Pierce to try and keep her safe, but it didn't save her. I stayed in that reality for a single day after her death before I reset it.

I tried again. I warned her, kept her safe, stayed by her at every waking second. We made it a single year before she was killed.

No matter what I tried, no matter what I effected, Jasmine Neck would not stay alive.

Resetting time became as normal as getting coffee. As normal as breathing.

I started to get better at keeping her alive, years would pass as I watched from the shadows. Getting involved always seemed to escalate things, so I stayed away.

The most frustrating part about my journey was never knowing who was killing her, and why. It was always different ways, different places. I refused to believe it was destiny. I felt it deep in my bones that my sister was not destined to die young.

My current reset, #13, I was watching Jaz from behind a bush. She and Alec were on a date. I still didn't like Alec very much, since he was completely useless at protecting her. Nothing had changed since my OG reality, it seemed.

"Wotcher," someone said beside me, and I shrieked, putting my hands over my mouth as I beheld a ghost.

"*What the fuck?*"

The transparent ghost furrowed his eyebrows at me, a shank of his long hair falling over his eyes. "Language, young lady. You are far too young to be using such foul words."

"Pfft, what are you, my dad? Fuck off. I only *look* like I'm fifteen. I'm really thirty-five."

"Well, I'm four hundred and one, milady."

I looked him up and down, seeing the magical threads woven into his tunic. "And yet, you don't look a day over two hundred."

He actually blushed at me, which was adorable for a ghost. Not that I'd ever seen one before. "You look like her." He tilted his chin towards where Jaz was across the street, holding Alec's hand. The ghost didn't appear to like seeing them together.

"Don't ask me why because I won't tell you," I informed him, and sat down on the grass.

"Very well, I won't tell you who I am either. Deal?"

I nodded.

"May I?" he asked, and I glanced up to see him reaching for my arm. I allowed him to hold it, and he tilted my forearm this way and that, looking at magic I couldn't see. I wondered what specialty he was. Elemental? "Tssk tssk, young witch. You've been messing with time. I can see it in your bones."

I took my arm back. "You would too if you knew why."

"I don't require an explanation. I assume it's valid, seeing the pain on your face, the blue in your hair. And her, of course." He watched her through the shrub, longing on his transparent face.

"Stop thirsting for my sister," I warned him.

"Pfft," he scoffed. "What are you, my dad?"

I laughed at him. It felt so nice to laugh. How long had it been?

"I'm Izzy," I told him as I offered my hand, and he shook it with his cold, ghostly palm.

"I'm Valentine."

✻ 4 ✻

Jaz

"Okay, whoa whoa, hold up," I interrupted. Sebastian shimmered into Gilbert, who looked like a deer in the headlights under my scowl. "Your name is *Valentine?* And my kind-of sister knew before I did?"

Goddess, this is some bullshit.

I turned to Pierce, shaking my finger at him. "And

you *died* so Izzy could reset time, you little bitch! We have discussed dying for me, and I am not having it."

"Jaz, dear, please let her finish," Pierce asked calmly, as he always did. Izzy had described him well.

"And *you*," I directed to Alec, pressing my finger to his nose, exactly the way Izzy said I used to do to her. "I will *murder* Candace if she ever touches you again."

Then I grabbed him and kissed him hard enough that he knew exactly who he belonged to.

I let him go, happily watching him shake his head to restart his brain, and sat back in my chair, folding my hands in front of me on the table. "Okay, you can keep going."

Izzy was still a little timid, as she had been throughout the retelling thus far, but she narrowed her eyes at Alec with more venom than I thought her capable of.

"I still don't like you, Alec," she informed him, and Bailey bristled at the thought of someone being in the room with her bae that bae didn't like. Izzy quieted her girlfriend with a hand on her arm.

"I understand," was Alec's response, and that made Izzy pause, confused as to why he wasn't fighting her opinion of him. "Please continue, Izzy."

I raised my hand. "Wait, I have a small question, if I might." Izzy nodded. "How many times have I been sucking fairy cock?"

"Ahh..." Her eyes darted to each of us, then back to me. "Never."

"Never?" Alec repeated.

She shrugged. "As far as I know."

Gilbert, or *Valentine*, shimmered back into Sebastian, and we just stared at each other for a few seconds. As many times as Izzy reset reality, he was never there. That was enough to make me teary eyed, not hearing about my death, or Pierce's death, or any of Izzy's story. Just knowing that I'd never loved him before now.

I looked up at the ceiling, wondering how long I had to wait before I could pretend I had a rogue eyelash so I could wipe my eyes. "Izzy, you can keep going. Please."

Izzy

VALENTINE CAME BACK MANY TIMES AFTER I RESET reality. He always seemed to be trailing after my sister, but never able to work up the courage to talk to her. He also absolutely *hated* seeing her other soulmates with her.

It seemed to work like clockwork now, after all this time. Pierce found her. Alec found her. Sometimes without my help, until they didn't need my prompting at all.

Over the years, I changed. I traded impulsiveness for patience. The heart inside me was old, but my face still looked young. Even so, I never forgot my mission. I never stopped trying to save Jasmine.

It was inevitable. When she died, our world died too. The beasts would overtake us, or humans would discover us, vampires would attack, or we'd destroy ourselves with our own hubris. One thing was achingly clear.

Witches would die without Jaz.

("No pressure," Jaz interjected at the table, before letting me continue.)

I had long since given up hope of speaking to my sister. I had to remain in her shadow, as I always had. The sun would stay in the sky, and I would follow after her.

After another unsuccessful attempt, I wandered through the halls of Highborn, waiting for the inevitable end of our world. Some of the teachers were still there, the few who had stayed behind to protect the school.

I chanced telling someone outside of our circle about my plight. Luckily, she was completely wasted, so I had no problem getting a prophecy out of the teacher.

I'd learned to not personally intervene in my sister's

life. I could work on subtle things, but coming to her never seemed to help, it always made things worse. So I wanted to see if there was a time, in any reality, in which I could come to Jaz, finally speak to her again. The witch's prophecy said that I could, provided a certain event happened first. I kept that prophecy close, giving me hope that one day this would end, and my sister would be safe.

Then came the reality that changed everything.

Jaz survived until she was eighteen. It rarely happened, and since I still didn't know why she was dying, I was in the dark how she had survived for so long.

When Jaz died in this reality... the darkness came from a new place. Someone I never expected.

Alec Claus destroyed the world.

Jaz

My mouth dropped open in shock. "You..." I pointed my finger at her, then at Alec. "He was evil. Evil Santa. Alec was *evil.*" I studied his face, picturing an evil grin overtaking his lips. What would that look like? What would he be like? I drummed my fingers on the table and hoped Pierce couldn't smell how aroused this was making me.

How hard would Evil Alec fuck me?

Alec just grinned at me, knowing me well enough to see where my head was at. "Enjoying this?"

"I'm not absolutely dripping wet at the thought of you being evil, totally not, don't be ridiculous."

"Gross," Izzy complained under her breath. "I can assure you, Evil Alec wasn't hot."

"Sis. You like girls. Alec is a *snack.*"

She rolled her eyes at me. "Anyway, as I was saying..."

Evil Alec role-play was on the docket for tonight.

Alec squeezed my arm so I'd focus when Izzy started talking again.

"The Claus estate had become the new royal palace," she said, using the same slightly dramatic tone as she had this entire time.

"I was the *king?*" Alec asked, interrupting her.

"Evil overlord, I'd say," she responded. "But yes, you went by Dark King Alec. There were t-shirts."

I snorted out a laugh. "Please tell me you kept one. I need it."

"How exactly did I become the Dark King Alec?" Soft and Squishy Fiancé Alec asked.

"You ahh..." Izzy chewed on her lip and drummed her fingers on the table exactly like I had been doing. "You kinda. Murdered the entire High Council."

Well shit.

"Because of..." He pointed to me, and Izzy shook her head.

"No. Because of him." She gestured to Pierce. "They had him publicly executed for being your husband."

"We were husbands??" Alec asked at the same moment Pierce said, "All we've done is kiss!"

"Could I... please..." Izzy said, patiently waiting for us to stop emoting all over her.

"Do please continue your tale of Pierce being my husbando," Alec encouraged while Pierce rolled his eyes and groaned.

Izzy

DARK KING ALEC HAD OVERTAKEN THE WITCH world. After losing not one, but two loves to his own kind, there was no stopping the darkness in his heart.

I had been doing this for a long time. Resetting reality was beginning to take its toll on me. I believed in my mission, I wanted to succeed, but there seemed no way to accomplish that.

I'd been alone for many years, without anyone to confide into after Valentine left my side. I came to the conclusion that I could no longer do this on my own. Not anymore.

I went to Dark King Alec for help.

The Claus estate had become a fortress, intent on keeping people out, but I had an advantage other people did not. I had his late wife's face. One call to the castle, and I was ushered in without comment. When I entered the castle, however, I discovered the real reason I'd been let in.

Valentine was there.

The Alec he stood next to was one I'd never seen before. His sadness had turned to unquenchable rage. I wanted to be upset that my sister's death wasn't the one to tip his scales, but Pierce was a good man, so I understood.

"Izzy," Alec greeted when I came in. "Valentine has told me a lot about you. Please, come in." They both led me to the sitting room where Alec poured us drinks and Valentine floated around the furniture.

"I haven't seen you in a while," I told the ghost while Alec handed me a glass.

Valentine sat on a chair near me, folding one leg over the other. "I decided to stay by Jaz's side after meeting you this time. I hope you've been well."

Actually, I'd been pretty fucking lonely, thanks for asking.

"So, you're the witch that's been fucking with time, making the demon portal weaker," Alec said as he sat on the sofa. "Valentine says you've been trying to keep our Jaz from dying, and you've been unsuccessful. Many. Many times."

I gulped down half of my drink. God, you have no idea how frustrating it had been to always be in an underage body. I missed margaritas. "That's correct."

I proceeded to tell him all that I've said up to now, and he merely listened, tapping his leg against the floor, and smoking a never-ending cigarette. I may not like Alec, but never let it be said that he's not the most intelligent warlock you'll ever meet.

("Aww," Alec cooed. "Sorry, but I'm engaged."

"Shut up," Jaz chastised.)

While he smoked that cigarette and drank enough alcohol to kill a horse, he contemplated the situation, long after I'd finished speaking. I drained my glass and almost nodded off before he spoke.

"You're doing it wrong," he said, and I raised an eyebrow at him.

"Gee, thanks. I didn't realize that after resetting time for fifty plus years."

He got up and waved at me in dismissal. "No. I mean, yes. You are doing it wrong. But also no. Because there's no way you could've known that you were doing it wrong. You're thinking of time as linear." He snapped his fingers and a glowing horizontal line appeared in front of us, courtesy of his Illusion specialty. "Here is where Jaz died, in your time." A vertical line crossed over the glowing line, right where Alec put his hand. "So you've been resetting time here." He made another vertical line, further up. "You assumed the problem started when you went to Highborn with Jaz, when you had that bad feeling on the train. But by that logic, you would've come up with a way to fix it by now. You would've seen who was behind this by now." He stuck his cigarette between his teeth and walked up the line, making a mark even further away. "We need to effect change *here*. A theoretical spot where Jaz's fate was sealed."

"But we don't know what that spot is," I told him, standing up to study the lines. "And I can't go further back, the youngest it's ever sent me back was nine. I'm sure you can imagine how hard it was to take care of myself that time, I don't want to *think* about being younger."

"You don't have to be younger."

He was insane.

("Hey!" Alec complained.)

Dark King Alec insisted he knew what to do. He took Valentine and me down to his secret laboratory, that honestly looked more like a sex dungeon, and he started working.

It took days to research, days to come up with a plan, and days for Alec to create new magic. I'd been around the block many times, and a warlock making new magic was almost unheard of, but he did it.

My Divination specialty helped create the spell, one that would work like a grenade once I reset time again. It would create a ripple effect, changing things further back than I could go, all with the intent on saving Jaz's life.

It was fueled by pure love.

Alec got the ingredients ready in a bowl, mixing it with his hands, and he looked up to check my rune work and Valentine's candle arrangement. "Valentine." The ghost looked up at him, setting a candle down. "This spell is powerful. It's new magic, it may affect us in the next reality."

"Affect us how?" I asked, but Alec set the bowl down and squared me with a dark look.

"You are not taking part, Isabelle. I won't risk anything happening to you so you can't reset time again. And most especially, if this harms us in the next reality, if it makes us weak or removes our ability to love, I can't do that to my wife's sister. Valentine and I will make the grenade, you will take it with you when you leave this reality."

"End of discussion," Valentine added for good measure, in case I felt like arguing. "And I will do anything to save her, Alec. I don't care what it costs."

Alec picked up the bowl, taking it over to my circle, and he met my eyes across it. "This will save Pierce too, yes? He'll come back to me?" I nodded, and Alec began.

I ONCE AGAIN HAD TO LEAVE A REALITY WITH BODIES lying beside me. Alec and Valentine weren't dead, no, just drained of every ounce of their magic. I wasn't sure that was something you could recover from, providing it didn't kill you.

As I readied my spell to reset time, I met Alec's weakened eyes, and he worked up a small smile.

"Save them, Izzy. Don't let my family die again."

With the grenade in hand, I reset time, and the men,

the laboratory, faded away as I shrank in height. Once the magic was gone, I set the grenade on the ground and it burst open, releasing the love of two men who were willing to die to save my sister.

There was nothing much left to do but wait after that.

When I first saw Jaz again, I knew something was different. The sunlight was gone from her eyes, she had become a shadow like me. The darkness encompassed her as the years passed, and it got harder and harder to watch.

Had Alec been wrong?

Then, one day, I crashed awake when I felt this reality be reset by someone else. By not me. And that had one terrifying consequence: I couldn't reset this reality again.

Alec and Valentine's grenade was still taking effect, still changing this new timeline, and all I had to do was wait to see if their love could break this cycle. If my sister could be saved.

☙ 5 ❧

Jaz

I zzy was still chewing her lip, she had to be biting it raw by now. "So, I think that brings you up to speed. Oh, I also met and fell in love with Bailey."

"You forgot the guys that are after you," Bailey mentioned, a pout settling on her gorgeous face.

"Ohh, right. That. Ahh... when this reality was reset with me in it, someone made an official report about the

47

reset, and the High Council decided to check up on things of that nature, and they discovered an alarm that had gone ignored, for obvious reasons. And that's how they found out about me."

"That's really bad, right?" Pierce asked.

She pressed her hands into her lap as Bailey put her arm across Izzy's chair. "Fucking with time is highly *highly* illegal for witches. I cannot even begin to express to you how illegal it is. There has to be a good reason, like how the reset for this one was to prevent the demon portal from exploding."

"But you reset time to save our world," Gilbert (Valentine) pointed out.

"No, I reset time to save my sister. I doubt they'll see it any other way. Especially when you consider that not all of my resets ended with witches losing, thanks to Alec." He beamed at her, like he was proud of himself. Izzy turned to Gilbert and tilted her head, studying his face. "It's a little weird seeing you... opaque. I always kinda pictured you with blue eyes."

Stop staring at him.

"So you forgot your name?" she asked.

Gil smiled down at her. "I don't remember anything about who I was before. All I remember is appearing when Jaz's magic went out. I couldn't speak to her, I could barely think. I just had to stay by her side."

"Seems like that might be the side effects Dark King

Me mentioned," Alec noted, looking quite dark at the thought. "I'm sorry about that, Gilbert. Err. Valentine?"

"Gilbert," he corrected with a small smile. "I prefer the name Jaz gave to me. And I am not sorry for the sacrifice. If what we did has even a shred of hope to save your life, Jaz, it was worth it."

Sebastian appeared with a soft smile on his blue face. "I'm one of those ripple changes, then. And Bailey too."

I wanted to be happy about that, but I was beginning to wonder what else was different this time around. What had been sacrificed to have Sebastian at my side?

"How..." Izzy blushed when I looked back at her again. She pointed to my hair. "How did your curls turn pink at the ends? You've never had that before."

I didn't really know how to answer as dread started to fill my body, but luckily, Alec spoke for me.

"It was when your father, Diego, died." Izzy fidgeted, peeking at me while I stared down at the table. "Did your father die in your other realities?"

Izzy opened and closed her mouth, then her voice came out shaky. "No. Only Jasmine. What... what happened to our father?"

Oh god. No, it couldn't be that. That was too much for me. I couldn't deal with having a new sister and reliving my dad's death at the same time, not after hearing everything she'd told me.

Had I traded my father for Sebastian?

I got up from the table and paced around the kitchen before pouring myself a cup of coffee that I nursed like a newborn baby.

"Could Jaz and I have a moment alone, please?" Izzy asked, her voice timid and sweet. She was the exact opposite of me.

"Izzy, I think it's best if we stay with her," Pierce said. "I apologize for being rude, but for the moment, we just would prefer to be cautious with Jaz, especially considering what you've just told us."

"I understand," she responded.

"I'll allow the rudeness," Bailey proclaimed, her arms crossed over her chest so everyone knew who was boss. "But don't do it again."

"*Bailey,*" Izzy admonished. "You promised to be nice."

"That's something my sister is not capable of," Sebastian noted dryly.

Bailey hopped up using her wings, bending over my blue lover with ire. "No one asked you, Sebastian. And you don't get to talk to my mate like that."

Alec tried to deescalate the two fairies as Sebastian stood and turned dark blue like he was holding his breath. "Could we please keep the sibling fights to a minimum? Like Pierce said, we're all family here." He pressed his hand to Sebastian's chest, and they shared a small look before Seb took a step back.

Stop stealing my lovers, Alec. Jesus.

Real talk, I loved watching them make out, but also real talk, I still wanted them all to myself.

"Bailey," Pierce said in his diplomatic way as he stood up, towering over everyone even though he was the shortest person at the table. "Maybe you're used to speaking to Sebastian like that in Fairyland, but we would appreciate it if you could try to get along with him while you're in our home. And Sebastian, I expect you to behave in a manner more befitting Jaz's household."

"*Excuse me?*" Sebastian ground out. "You aren't the Head Soulmate, Pierce. You don't get to order me around. I rescind the kisses I gave you before."

Oh my god, did we all have the Willies again?

"Actually, he *is* the Head Soulmate now," Alec said out of the blue, making us all stop. "I gave the position over to him earlier, before Izzy arrived. I didn't get a chance to tell you. I am sorry, Jaz."

There's only one reason he would've done that, given up his position in my household, and that's because he believed himself to be compromised. His sloppy resurrection was going to fail. We didn't know when, but it was going to happen.

Izzy looked so confused and lost. "Why would you give up your position, Alec?"

"Alright," I declared, slamming my cup onto the

counter. "This is how this is going to go. I'm going outside for a walk, and I'd like Izzy to come with me. Everyone else can pack a bag, we're going to my parents' house in the morning. Or..." I met her eyes, holding in my shudder. "...*our* parents' house."

She smiled so sweetly. *Was she actually related to me???*

Izzy followed me outside the Soulmate dorm, the moon lighting our journey across the lawn. She trotted beside me while I made long strides, an unconscious thought so we could get this over with.

"Jaz, slow down. God, you were always doing that when we were little. I can never keep up with you."

Grunting, I slowed down and she caught up with me, then I shuddered again as I looked over at her. "I feel very weird right now, Izzy. You just..." I mimicked an explosion with my hands. "You exploded my life. I don't know how to process this at all."

Her smile was so patient. So loving. She was the exact opposite of me. "I understand. I know I'm coming on strong, I just..." Blinking, she looked down at our shoes in the grass. When she met my eyes again, tears were streaming down her cheeks. "I've missed you *so much*. I've lived decades in your shadow, and I could never speak to you. I thought I never would again."

It was hard to think with her crying, and I resisted the urge to just hug her tears away. I squared my jaw, straightened my spine, and she seemed to recognize this pose because she stopped sniffing and waited for me to talk.

"Before we go forward with our relationship, before I start accepting all of this and getting used to having a sister, I have something I need to say to you. You might cry, but I need to say it." I let out a slow breath and she wiped her cheeks. "You put the men I love at risk to save my life. I understand why, I really do, Izzy. Truly. But I can't have that anymore. Not now, not ever. Our father died in front of me. Alec died in front of me. I won't go through that ever again." Now I was the one crying, before she could work her tears up again. "Izzy, our mom has lived for thirteen years without dad, without her soulmate. We both have soulmates now, I don't have to tell you how empty and devastating that must feel for her. But I know how it feels, and I can't do it again. You have to promise me that you will keep them safe too. Especially..." I swallowed, my throat painfully thick. "Especially if I don't make it."

She nodded, trying to smile behind the tears coursing down her cheeks. "I'm sorry, Jazzy."

I choked at her stupid nickname and tears blew off my nose. "What are you sorry for?"

"I begged you," she said hoarsely. "I begged you to stay on the train. I can't tell you how many times I've replayed that day, thinking that your death was my fault. If I'd just kept you there, maybe you would've been safe.

Everything that's happened after that was because of me."

I wanted to grab her in a hug, but I kept my arms firmly by my sides.

"You hush your whore mouth, Izzy," I reprimanded through more tears, and she sobbed out a laugh. "Alec proved this had nothing to do with that day. You aren't to blame at all, you hear me? But..." I glared at her, all warmth gone from my face, making her eyes widen. "You hurt my men, and I *will* blame you."

Her shock melted and she smiled at me. "The same goes for my Bailey. Please protect her."

I motioned for her to follow, and we kept walking into the night. "Bailey is a force of nature, I couldn't protect her if I tried. She's also really cute, by the way."

Izzy giggled and stared up at me as we walked over a log. "I thought you didn't like girls. You've never liked girls before."

I shrugged, not bothering to deny how hot I found that little pink skinned beauty, despite the fact that she'd gladly flay me alive. "Meh. I'm just super chill now, like Pierce. He's also mine, no more kissing."

"Bleck, I don't want to kiss him."

"Good."

Izzy

I stayed out with my sister for hours, just talking about our lives. I may have watched her from a distance for years, but there were still things I didn't know about her. I could've spent days getting to know her again, having her get to know me.

We were both tired from staying up, so we went back

to the soulmate dorm, creeping into her apartment in case everyone had gone back to sleep.

Jaz stopped me before I'd left the welcome rug. "Shoes off. Pierce's customs are important to us, so we go barefoot in our home, and we eat Kimchi." She watched me take my shoes off and we both put ours onto the shoe rack with everyone else's.

Bailey's shoes were still there, but the living room seemed empty, and the lights had been dimmed so only Jaz's salt lamp lit the room. Before I could start to worry, Bailey's purple head poked up from the couch and she smiled at me sleepily as her pink wings fluttered behind her.

"Hey beautiful," she greeted, making my stomach flutter in time with her wings. "You good, baby?"

I walked to the couch, leaning down to kiss her pink lips, and feeling warm all over from being close to her. "You didn't have to wait up."

Finding Bailey was the best thing that had ever happened to me. What had I ever done to deserve her?

Jaz whistled to get our attention, as we were completely absorbed in each other. "Be warned, Alec is a perv, which I'm sure you both know by now. He can and will listen in, so no hanky panky on the couch. Sorry to be a buzz kill." She came closer, just barely glancing at Bailey before looking back at me. "Izzy. We're safe, right? No one is coming after you right now?"

Bailey got up onto her knees so she could put her pink arms around my waist. "I'm using fairy magic to keep them away. They won't find her as long as I'm here. And I'm not leaving Izzy's side. Ever." I leaned down and kissed her purple hair, putting my arms around her neck, holding her close. "And if Alec listens in on us, he may find himself castrated."

"*Bailey!*" I chided, pulling her face back so I could meet her eyes. "We're not hurting anyone, not even Alec."

She grumped under her breath, but nodded in agreement. Jaz left us in the living room and when her bedroom door closed, I pet Bailey's head with a smile.

"My little murder queen, willing to do anything to keep me happy," I purred for her.

My fairy sat up more until she was leaning over me, tilting my chin up with her manicured finger. "You're not allowed to be adorable if I can't fuck you."

I grinned my most adorable grin. "Too late."

Bailey pounced. She tugged me off my feet and onto the couch, helping me straddle her hips. I bucked against her as her fingers slid down my stomach and slipped into my panties, swirling around my wet center until she found my swollen bud.

"Sssssh," she whispered when I couldn't hold in my moan. I bit my lip, unable to keep from squealing as she rubbed my clit with her fingertip.

"I can't..." I gasped and bit my lip further. "I can't keep quiet with you doing that." I got lightheaded from her touch, craving more of it, not even caring that someone could hear.

She leaned up, nuzzling my ear, taking the lobe between her teeth. "That's the idea."

For someone who hated the thought of anyone watching us, she sure liked flirting with danger.

Her fingers stilled and I almost fell on top of her from the shock. "Want me to stop?"

To counteract her teasing, I slid myself up and down her finger, riding it as hard as I wanted to ride her body. She liked the change, her eyes cloudy with desire. Her free hand floated around me, tugging on my hair, then gripping my hip as I rode her finger, rubbing my clit against it, desperately seeking climax.

I took her hand, sliding it between us, slipping both our hands into her panties. "Come with me, Bailey." She was so wet, slick with need, desperate for my touch. While her fingers rubbed her clit, I slid mine down and pressed inside her, curling to reach her pleasure spot. I knew the moment I found it, when her face squeezed in pleasure, her legs twitching underneath me.

"*Fuck*," she exclaimed, a little too loud for comfort, and I hushed her with a deep kiss, eating her moans up like a cupcake.

I was too focused on her pleasure to remember my

own, my body starting to crest without me realizing it. Her little pink finger started pulling a climax from me, and I furiously thrust inside her until she was coming too, squirting all over my hand, whimpering in my mouth. Releasing her lips, I eagerly looked into her eyes to watch the fading embers of her orgasm, giving her a few last thrusts that made her throw her head back and shake against me.

That's my girl.

Removing our hands, I fell on top of her and lay against her breasts, feeling her erratic breathing start to even out after a few minutes, in time with my own. She lifted a weak hand and stroked my blue curls, humming softly to me as I closed my eyes.

It had been so long since someone else took care of me. I barely knew what it felt like before Bailey entered my life, and she instantly became my protector. My lover. My best friend. My family.

My breath hitched in thought and Bailey brought her other arm up to hold me close.

"You're nervous about seeing them, aren't you?" she whispered into the darkened living room. I nodded against her, unable to form words for how I was feeling. "I'll protect you. I'm never leaving your side, Izzy. Not ever. Even if you're gone from this reality, if it gets reset again, if something happens. I will always find you."

I wanted to be comforted. But I'd lived for too long,

seen too much, and the fact that this was the first reality I'd found her in, I wasn't sure I'd find her again if something happened, and that terrified me so much I could barely breathe.

"You don't believe me?" She tucked a finger under my chin and lifted my head, capturing me with her piercing pink gaze. Lying underneath her body, her wings started glowing, filling with fairy magic. "*Oh magic, deep within. A bond must be made, a bond of kin. No time, or space, or reality, can take this witch away from me. Our memories shared will always stay, even should this reality decay. Bind our magic together as one, once this spell is complete and done.*"

Her pink magic swirled around me, slipping inside my body, mixing with my own pool of magic. The pool accepted it, loved it, and filled me with reassurance.

I sealed our spell with a kiss.

"I love you, Bailey," I whispered against her lips, before kissing her over and over, tears of happiness running down my cheeks.

She flipped us until she was on top of me, her wings fluttering behind her, filling the room with pink light. "I love you. I will always love you, my beautiful Izzy."

7

Jaz

In the early morning, I woke first this time. Usually, I woke to an empty bed because my lovers were already up making breakfast and getting ready for our day. But today, I was the first to open their eyes.

Alec lay in front of me, his shirtless body making me drool. Sebastian had a blue arm around the warlock in his sleep, murmuring something in Fairy. Pierce held me from behind, pressing his thick body against me. This had to be my favorite way to wake up, being held by Pierce as I stared into Alec's handsome face.

Sebastian stirred, as if sensing that I was awake, peeping up over Alec's shoulder and smiling sleepily at me. He climbed over the warlock and snuggled his head against my stomach, holding me around my hips. Alec pressed closer, resting our foreheads together.

Never mind. *This* was my favorite way to wake up.

Alec moaned sleepily and stretched his legs out. "Early morning sexies?" He grabbed at me, grunting when I moved further into Pierce's body to get away from him.

"No, my sister is in the other room."

Pierce snorted, kissing my bare shoulder. "That didn't stop them last night. Sorry, couldn't help it, wolf hearing and all. Not the most traumatizing experience I've had, sadly."

"I'd advise you to keep that to yourself, Bailey might skin you alive," Sebastian warned against my stomach.

"Noted," Pierce affirmed, holding me tighter.

I noticed Alec was pouting at me. "What's wrong? *Is Santa angwee about the no sex? Wiww I be on the naughty wist, UwU?*"

He narrowed his eyes at me. "What is wrong with you?"

"Like... right now? Or in general. Those are two different answers."

His growl made me wetter than the ocean.

Then he got up and the other two followed suit, leaving me a dripping mess on the bed. RUDE. Grumping, I got up, looking around for my familiar, Merlin, as I grabbed my phone from the nightstand.

"Merlin? Pspsps," I called, bending to check under the bed.

"He's not a cat," Pierce reminded me as he covered up his gloriousness with a shirt. Fucking shirts, ruining my view.

Sebastian helped me by checking the wardrobe and under the pillows. "I haven't seen him, darling. Maybe he went to the kitchen?"

"He rarely leaves Jaz, that is a bit..." Alec froze as Astella's little nose peeped out from his collar. His familiar, a pink fairy armadillo, was very attached to my pygmy Tarsier. If he wasn't with me, he was usually with her. "Oh shit," Alec swore under his breath, and he left the room, going down the hallway to the kitchen.

I followed behind, thinking maybe Astella clued him in on Merlin's whereabouts, when I came into the room and beheld the worst betrayal of my entire life.

Merlin was sitting on Izzy's shoulder.

That little whore was sitting there, contentedly

watching Izzy cook something over the stove, like this was a normal day.

If I could be like my mom and turn bright red as I burn the apartment building down, I would've done so.

"SHE'S NOT MOMMY, I'M MOMMY!"

Izzy jumped and Merlin's already wide eyes went even wider.

But Mommy, he started as I squinted at him. *Merlin like her too.*

"Jaz!" Izzy said with a smile as she turned to me, holding a pan of skillet cinnamon rolls. "Sorry, Merlin came up to me a few hours ago. He's been telling me all about how you found him at the zoo, how happy you've made him. I think he just wanted to get to know me."

I put my hand out and Merlin jumped back to me, snuggling against my neck where I clutched him close to me. Having someone else touch him was like having my teeth pulled, I couldn't stand it.

Izzy set the pan down and wiped her hands on her apron. "Sorry, I didn't mean to upset you. I know how people can be about their familiars." I pet Merlin with one finger, eyeing my twin with scrutiny. "I thought I could never be more jealous of you, but I am. I've wished for a long time that I could have a familiar, someone to be with me throughout everything. You're lucky to have him."

Bailey came up to her, wrapping her arms around my

sister's waist, kissing her neck. "I'll be your familiar," she purred, exactly the way Sebastian liked to purr when he touched me, her wings fluttering around behind her.

"Eww," I grumped, curling my nose. Bailey glowered at me so I'd shut up.

"You don't need a pet now, I'll stay with you forever," she whispered to Izzy, and they shared a sweet look over Izzy's shoulder, nuzzling their noses together. As nauseating as it was to see my sister doing that, their love was adorable as fuck.

I brought Merlin up to my face and pointed a finger at him. "You're *my* baby. Benedict Merlin."

Mommy is best mommy. He made a little anime 'chu' sound, trying to be as adorable as possible. My little one knew exactly how to diffuse me.

"Damn straight," I told him with a snuggle.

Pierce came up behind me and held me like Bailey was holding my sister, resting his chin on my shoulder. "And you said your maternal instincts are shit."

Sniffing, I tucked Merlin into my boobs where he cuddled in my bra as he usually did. I was starting to feel weird when my little Tarsier wasn't under my boobs.

Izzy served us all cinnamon rolls, giving Bailey an extra one and a kiss on the fairy's purple head. Izzy danced around the kitchen like a 1950's housewife, twirling her apron as she set the enchanted cleaning sponge out to take care of the dishes while we sat down to eat.

Magician's taint. Her cinnamon rolls were fucking amazing. Even Alec went silent as he chewed a large mouthful of them, and he usually used breakfast to make as many sex comments as possible, just in case I missed his potty mouth during school.

Bailey unhinged her jaw to shove an entire cinnamon roll into her pink mouth, and she moaned loudly enough that Pierce started turning red. *"Ohmygodddd,* fucking marry me, you sexy little witch. I want you to cook me cinnamon rolls every morning, wearing only that apron. Naked Izzy in my kitchen, mmm."

We all collectively choked on our food.

Sebastian squared his sister with a look, and she just stared back, chewing her massive bite of food. "Bailey, for real. I am *eating.* Would you like me talking like that? Do you want me to remind everyone that I have specific plans to fuck both Jaz and Alec on this table? I'm going to make Alec come all over it. Shall I continue?"

Izzy's eyes widened into saucers and she picked her plate up, just in case the table was tainted. "Please no. Bailey, chill. We talked about this."

The pink fairy grumped, but agreed with her bae to cool it.

Alec, on the other hand, was blushing up to his ears, staring at our table like it held the secrets to life. He flicked his eyes up to the blue fairy, and Sebastian puckered up with a wink.

Taking a long sip of my coffee, I sat back in my chair and shut my eyes. Mmmm. Magic bean juice. "Reminder that we are about to go to my parents' house. You can't make sex comments about fucking their daughters at the table."

"We will all be on our best behavior," Pierce promised, giving everyone else a look that meant they'd better fall in line. My sexy Alpha wolf being all in charge. I would've said something about how hot he was being, but I decided to spare Izzy from picturing me riding Lycan cock. Not to mention, he was still turning bright red whenever my sister looked at him.

What exactly did he hear last night?

We finished eating and Izzy went to the bathroom with Bailey right behind her. Was she peeing with Bailey in there? Eww! I may not have a lot of boundaries with my guys, given they regularly fucked my ass, but that was a hard pass for me. I don't care if the season finale to Grey's Anatomy is happening, I pee with the door *closed.*

"So..." I started, tapping my fingers against my mug as I stared at Pierce. "You keep blushing when you look at the girls, honey buns. And I'm not talking about my tits."

"She ahh..." He sighed and rolled his eyes towards

the ceiling. "Izzy's moans sound exactly like yours. It's hard to get out of my head."

"Never mind, I regret saying anything. Hands off my sister, you're *mine*." I pointed a finger at him, and swirled it around to the other two. "That includes everybody else at this table. She has my face, but *I'm* the hot one." My eyes shifted towards the bathroom door, and I flipped back to my conversation with Izzy last night. "There's another thing we should talk about, and I want to say it while we have a moment alone."

Pierce reached across the table to me, holding my hand in his. "You can tell us anything. We're right here to listen." Alec and Sebastian put their hands on top of ours, with Gilbert shimmering in and out to let me know he was there.

"Izzy's story has me terrified. It's not my death that bothers me, it's that all of you sacrificed for me. I know Sebastian wasn't included in that, but he would be if he'd been in our lives before." I set my jaw to hold back my emotions. "I will not live without any of you. And don't you dare use my ability to resurrect as a cop out to jump in front of a bullet for me. No dying. No sacrifices. I've warned Izzy as well to not use you the way she did before, because I just can't deal with it if any of you are hurt."

Alec removed his hand, making my heart stop. "I'm not promising that. I'm sorry if that hurts you, but I won't." Before I could say anything, he twisted my chair and leaned over to hold me in his arms, encompassing me with the musky scent of his jacket. "I would die a thousand times to keep you safe. If anyone hurts you, I will reduce them to ashes. And I've said it before, I will repeat it every day of our lives. Even if I die, I will not leave your side. So please..." He tugged on my hair, clasping me as close as he could. "Don't make me promise that I won't save you."

Damn you, Alec. My tears splashed onto his vest, and I desperately clutched him, feeling as if I'd fall apart if I left his arms.

Someone grabbed me from his arms, pulling me up, capturing my lips in a forceful kiss. Alec pressed into me from behind, grasping my waist, and Pierce came up to the side, holding me there too. When I opened my eyes, it was Gilbert holding me, tugging me up on my tiptoes.

"We're not promising shit, Jaz," he told me. "We're putting you first, end of discussion. If anything, Izzy's story just confirmed that you need us to keep you safe, and that's exactly what we'll be doing. So, suck it."

Pierce gently took me over, pressing our foreheads together. Anyone else would've stood up on their tip toes so I had to look up at them, but not Pierce. I was always on equal footing with him, literally and figuratively. "I know you don't want to lose us. I know it's your biggest fear, and we would never intentionally make that fear a reality. We're brothers now. And we'll keep our mate safe, as well as each other."

"Brothers," Alec commented. "I don't want to kiss my *brothers*. Could you use a better term?"

Pierce narrowed his eyes, surprising everyone when he yanked on Alec's tie until the warlock was leaning over him. Then he kissed Alec right on the lips. "Shut the fuck up."

Alec straightened, looking a little dizzy. "Yep. Shutting up." Pierce looked pleased with himself as Alec fluffed his hair and fixed his tie with a flush on his fancy boi cheeks.

Fucking Christ, was this my life now? *Thank you, life. You're the best.*

8

Izzy

After I washed up with a cloth and changed my clothes, Bailey watched me as I pinned up half of my hair. She sat on the toilet lid, just watching me exist.

"You good, Iz?"

I nodded to her, checking my hair for stray curls

before putting everything back into my Eevee bag. "Bailey." She straightened her back like an excited puppy when I addressed her. "Best behavior. I adore your guard dog act, I really do. But I need you to tone it down just a smidge. And please, *please*, get along with your brother. I don't want Jaz to not like having me around."

Bailey's wings fluttered, betraying her annoyance despite the placid look on her face. "I understand. I'm sorry that I come on too strong. I'm not going to stop being a mama bear, so everyone will have to deal." I raised an eyebrow at her. "Anddd... I'll get along with Sebastian. Happy?"

I came to her, putting my hands on her shoulders. "I love who you are. You fight for me, no one has done that since I lost my sister the first time. But now they're all in our corner, so we need to let them in." I slid my thumb along her chin, tilting her head up. "Could you do that please? For me?"

She pulled me close, resting her head on my stomach. "Yes. I'd do anything for you. Except a threesome. I refuse to share you."

An image briefly flitted through my mind, of me wrapped around Bailey, and my long time popstar crush, Aurora.

Bailey tightened her hold on me. "You're thinking about *her* aren't you? Betrayal."

"Didn't realize you read minds, that's cute."

She stood up, my pink fairy towering over me. Now she was the one tilting my chin, asserting her dominance over me with a single grin. "*Mine.*" I gulped, desire over-riding my brain. "The next time you think of someone else when you're in my arms, I'm bending you over my knee, Isabelle Neck."

I just might do it on purpose, then, I thought defiantly.

Bailey took my hand and walked me out of the bathroom. Jaz and her men were putting their shoes on at the door, so we did the same, and walked out into the hallway.

A door opened further down and two girls came out. Bailey instantly stood in front of me to block their view, so I peeped through her arm to see a mousy girl holding hands with a scary looking girl.

"Jaz! I'm so glad we caught you. We just wanted to apologize for everything that happened, we know we made you worry about us during the Willies outbreak." Mousy girl leaned over and waved at me from behind Bailey. "Who's your friends... omg! Jaz, you didn't tell us you had a *twin sister!*"

"I thought you were an only child," scary girl commented as she tugged mousy girl closer to her. "Your grandparents advertised you as their only living grand-child at your debut party."

"Debut party?" I asked, turning to Jaz.

"Those motherfuckers," she ground out. "Our older cousin is very much so alive, I can't *believe* those two..." She steeled herself with a deep breath. "Sorry, ahh... This is Izzy, my sister, and her girlfriend, Bailey. Girls, this is Pollyanna and Andi, our dorm mates. Izzy was umm... we were separated at birth. We didn't know she existed. Until now, that is."

"Oooo! Very 'Parent Trap,' I love it!" Pollyanna waved to me again as Bailey tried desperately to keep me hidden. "Hello, Izzy! Oooo, Bailey you are very lovely. I've never seen a fairy before. Nice to meet you both." She held out her hand, but Andi grabbed both of her arms to keep her pinned.

All these soulmates and their jealous possession of us. There wasn't a single soulmated couple here that didn't have one marshmallow person and one overprotective person who hated people even *looking* at their lover.

I was the marshmallow in this relationship.

Jaz

My flying Cadillac just barely fit all of us. Izzy and Bailey were in the front with me, and my four guys were in the back, all grumping that they couldn't sit next to me.

"Ooo, fancy!" Izzy cooed from the middle front seat. She pressed a few buttons to turn on witch radio, filling the car with old timey jazz music.

"Alec gave it to me, it was his father's favorite car." I met his eyes in the rearview mirror, sharing a smile over it.

"Always happy to please my lady, and piss my dad off at the same time." He winked, and a thrill went up my spine.

I put the car in gear and bent to check the window as I backed out of the Highborn parking garage, just barely catching Gilbert's eye before I had to focus. "We won't all fit in here soon, you know. We'll have to think of a solution."

Izzy tilted her head at me. "What do you mean? Who's joining us later? Are you getting another boyfriend, Jaz?"

The back seat yelled out a firm "no" as an answer.

"She means when she resurrects Gilbert," Alec explained. "We have to find his body first, and Jaz has to work up her skills—"

"Wait," Izzy interrupted, turning in her seat to look at me. "You're a *necromancer?*"

I stole glances at her as I watched the road, driving through Highborn Village. "Well, yeah. Don't tell me you watched me for fifty-odd years and never knew that."

She burst out crying.

Bailey shot daggers at me, but remained calm as she pat Izzy on the back. "Could we please *not* make Izzy cry?" That was downright the most civil thing she'd said since we met.

"Izzy, why are you upset? I wasn't trying to be mean." I couldn't drive and console her at the same time.

"I..." She held in a sob and pushed her blue curls back. "I used to dream of the next necromancer, hoping they could bring you back. I mentioned that last night."

"I remember," I said, almost hitting a wall with the car when I checked on her.

"But *you* were the next necromancer the entire time."

"She can't exactly bring herself back to life," Gilbert cheeked, and Izzy giggled as she wiped her tears.

"Could you show me?" she asked, meeting my eyes when I stopped at a stop sign.

"I'm driving."

"No, not right now. I just want to see. I..." Izzy squeezed my hand on the steering wheel. "I'm so proud of you, Jaz. I've felt guilty for so long that I found my specialty and you didn't. And look at you, you got the rarest most special gift of all."

Blushing, I kept driving and she took her hand back. "Damn straight. But for real though, you never saw me specialize before, or practice my magic?" She shook her head. "Hmm. That's a little weird. But I mean, you weren't there the entire time, right? I tend to resurrect in secret." I met Alec's eyes in the rearview, revealing he thought the same as me.

Izzy should've seen me specialize, or practicing necromancy, at the very least. There's no way she could've been by my side for so long and missed that.

Was she lying about who she was?

Should I trust her at all?

I CHEWED MY LIP TO RIBBONS DURING THE DRIVE TO my parents' house. Izzy made conversation, but I couldn't add to it, not with the growing fear inside me. If Izzy's stories didn't add up, how was I supposed to handle that? She'd just cry and Bailey would kill me.

Pulling up in front of my childhood home, Alec and I shared another look in the mirror before I got out and met the girls on the sidewalk. My soulmates took the next few moments to have a quick talk, then they joined us too.

Alec immediately came to my side, putting his hand on my back and kissing my forehead to calm me. "I texted your parents, but they don't know why we're here yet. I figured this was an in-person conversation."

Everyone started up the sidewalk, but I curled into Alec's body, tucking my arms underneath his jacket.

"You're safe," he whispered, bending his head over me. "If she's lying, I won't let her hurt you."

I always felt safe in Alec's arms, but I didn't feel calm. I needed my calm. I needed Sebastian. He was there before I could move, folding me against him, his big blue chest resting against my cheek. Taking my hand, he led me up the sidewalk with Alec holding my other hand and Pierce taking the back.

"I need more hands," I told them under my breath, and Sebastian snorted out a laugh.

Izzy was smiling as she waited for us near the door, and I could see her anxiety as she tapped her foot against the sidewalk. So we were both on edge, and about to see our volatile mother who has set the house on fire before when she got pissed off.

Perfect.

The enchanted doorknob opened for me, as a member of the Neck household, and I held it open for everyone to come inside. We stood in the great room, the living and dining area combined in one space. Izzy grabbed one of the chairs and held it in her hands, squeezing the wood.

"I haven't been here for *so long*," she whispered. Her head shot up when someone came down the stairs.

"Jasmine? Is that you?" Bosley, dad #2, walked in wearing his house robe, a typical outfit for him when he didn't have to leave the house. He was all smiles until he spotted Izzy, and he went pale, taking a step back. "Jasmine. Who is that?"

Aldrich, dad #3, was right behind him. He stayed silent when he saw Izzy, equally shocked, but holding it in. My mom entered the room last, and everyone held their breath.

When my mom went still, it was usually a bad sign, and my pulse shot up as I watched her just standing there, staring at Izzy like she was a ghost.

Swallowing down my fear about her, I stepped up, took her hand, and led her to our parents. "Mom. Dads. This is Izzy. She's my twin. I know it's obvious, I just wanted to say it."

"Baby... you don't have a twin," Bosley said.

"We were all there when you were born, darling. There's no way..." Aldrich twisted his head at her, trying to see the magic around Izzy.

Mom was the first to move, standing in front of us, putting her hand on Izzy's cheek. "Isabelle. That's your name, isn't it?" Izzy nodded. "Twins run in my family, Diego's as well. We assumed we would have twins. We picked out two names. But..."

"You only had one baby," Izzy finished for her, her voice trembling.

With her eyebrows knitting together, Mom took a strand of Izzy's blue hair between her fingertips. "How did this happen to you?" She asked like it was a scar, a battle wound, which, in a way, I guess it was. Then Mom straightened, clasping her robe to keep her hands busy. "I'll make some tea. I'd like to hear your story, Isabelle."

ONCE EVERYTHING WAS SAID, WE SAT AT THE PATIO table, sipping tea and trying to process. Hell, I'd heard the story twice now and I was still processing.

Mom got up, taking the teapot from the table. "I'll get more tea."

I followed after her, coming into the kitchen where she stood at the sink, pouring water into the tea kettle. "Mom."

She tilted her head in my direction but kept her eyes on the water. "I... I've lived for so long, feeling like my life was empty. That the only meaning I had was you. I held onto that, it was my sword in every battle my mind tried to win." Her hands shook as she turned the faucet off. "And now I find out that I've not only lost a daughter, Diego's death was the price to keep my girls safe."

"Do you resent that?"

Mom dropped the kettle and turned on me so fast, I almost took a step back. "Jasmine Sofia Neck."

Fuck me.

"You look at me right in the eyes, young lady. I would sacrifice everything I have to keep you alive. Your fathers would as well, all three of them. If this is why I lost Diego, I would pay that price again and again." Mom wrapped me in her embrace, filling me with the herbal scent of her soap. She always smelled like a garden. "I know it's been hard watching me all these years. My pain is hard to hide. But I could never resent you for anything, you did nothing wrong. And if Diego knew that dying would protect you, he would've made that sacrifice without a second thought."

As she ran her fingers through my unruly curls, the only thought that filled my head was making this right. Her eyebrows raised as the thought formed in my head and telegraphed straight to her mind.

I didn't need to say it out loud after she read my thoughts, but I did, just to reaffirm my intentions. "A demon said I can't resurrect Dad. His cremation makes it impossible." Her hand stilled, then she kept stroking my hair. I bent up to look at my mom. "I'm going to find a way. I can bring Dad back."

My mom's eyes shifted through so many emotions, I could barely pick a single one out of the pool. "I don't have to tell you what that would mean to me. But you make sure you're safe first before you try. And if you can't..." She squeezed my shoulders, and she put on a brave face. "I'll see him again someday."

"I appreciate the bravado, Mom, but you boss me about everything else, you can boss me about the one thing that matters to you." She started scowling at me. "After me, of course. And..." I turned my head, staring out at Izzy as she laughed at something. "Maybe her too."

"Fine. You're finding a way to resurrect your father, or you don't get dessert."

I high fived her. "There ya go."

WE ATE DINNER AND EVERYONE WENT TO BED. IZZY and Bailey were in the spare room, while I was in my old room, lying on my big bed with my four lovers. I'd turned on my enchanted stone that projected the night sky onto my ceiling, and we lay there staring up at it, the stars flitting across our faces.

Izzy's recap of all she'd told us just had me feeling

more uncomfortable. How could she have missed why I kept dying? Nothing was making sense.

"I don't know how to feel about any of this yet," I said as a galaxy passed by my face.

"None of us do," Pierce reassured me, clasping my hand. Sebastian took my other hand, and the boys finished the circle between themselves. Our magic floated above the bed, intertwining between our bodies, a connection that bound us together.

"We'll figure it out. We always do." Alec bumped my head with his since he couldn't reach me, caressing me with his skull.

Sebastian squeezed my hand. "Jasmine. My sister may not be the nicest person, but she has a good head on her shoulders. If she trusts Izzy, then I do as well." I almost relaxed, but he kept going. "Unless she's fucking with me again, but I highly doubt it. She wouldn't put me in danger."

"You suck at comforting people," Gilbert noted as he flitted in and out. "Izzy's powerful. She's the twin of a necromancer, she's stronger than any witch we've seen. She's stronger than *Alec*."

Alec beamed with pride, making a cute noise in his throat. "I like compliments better when there's a hand on my cock."

Gilbert smacked him. "Shush, you thirsty turnip. If

Izzy turns on us, we can't take her down. That's a fact. The safest thing is to trust her. For now."

"For now," I echoed, and shut my eyes as the galaxy overtook me, drifting me away with the men I loved.

End of book four

Book Five in the Neck-Romancer Series
Neck-Rotic

ABOUT THE AUTHOR

Photo by Elizabeth Dunlap

Elizabeth Dunlap is the author of several fantasy books, including the Born Vampire series. She's never wanted to be anything else in her life, except maybe a vampire.

You can find her online at
www.elizabethdunlap.com

facebook.com/edunlapnifty

twitter.com/edunlapnifty

instagram.com/edunlapnifty

goodreads.com/Elizabeth_Dunlap

bookbub.com/authors/elizabeth-dunlap

amazon.com/author/ElizabethDunlap

tiktok.com/edunlapnifty